Weed was a big seed.
Rose was a seed, but
Rose was not as big as
Weed.

A man had a pot.
The man dug a deep
hole in the pot.

The man set Rose in
the deep hole.
But he did not see
Weed get in the hole.

The man got a hose.
"I need to keep the
seed wet," said the
man.

"I need to keep the
pot in the sun," said
the man.
So the man set the pot
in the sun.

Late in the week, a
bug got into the pot.
The bug met Rose and
Weed.

Rose had a leaf, but
Weed had a big leaf.

In a week, Weed got big.
Rose did not seem to
get big.

"I am a big weed,"
said Weed.
"Rose is not big."
Weed made Rose
feel sad.

"Do not make fun of
Rose," said the bug.
"I need to get big,"
said Rose.

"I can feel the sun,"
said Rose.
In time, the sun did
make Rose big, but
not as big as Weed.

The bug got on a big
leaf.
"Take a peek at Rose,"
said the bug.
"I see a bud."

"Keep it up, Rose,"
said the bug.
"It is a fine bud."

The bud got big.
It made a big, red rose.
Rose did not feel sad.

"I see," said Weed.
"I am a big weed,
but a rose is not
the same as a weed."

"A weed can get big,"
said the bug.
"But a weed can not
make a fine, red rose."